BEFORE I GO TO SLEEP

by **Thomas Hood**

illustrated by
Maryjane Begin-Callanan

G.P. Putnam's Sons   New York

Illustrations copyright © 1990 by Maryjane Begin-Callanan
All rights reserved. This book, or parts thereof,
may not be reproduced in any form
without permission in writing from the publisher.
G. P. Putnam's Sons, a division of
The Putnam & Grosset Group,
200 Madison Avenue, New York, NY 10016.
Published simultaneously in Canada.
Printed in Hong Kong by South China Printing Co. (1988) Ltd.
Typography by Christy Hale
Library of Congress Cataloging-in-Publication Data
Hood, Thomas.
Before I go to sleep/by Thomas Hood:
illustrated by Maryjane Begin-Callanan. p.   cm.
Summary: Before falling asleep, a child imagines
being a variety of animals.
ISBN 0-399-21638-3
[1. Bedtime—Fiction. 2. Imagination—Fiction.
3. Animals—Fiction. 4. Stories in rhyme.]
I. Begin-Callanan, Maryjane, ill. II. Title.
PZ8.3.H758Wh 1990 88-11443 CIP AC   [E]—dc19
1 3 5 7 9 10 8 6 4 2
First Impression

To Brian

In the summer when I go to bed
The sun still streaming overhead
My bed becomes so small and hot
With sheets and pillow in a knot,
And then I lie and try to see
The things I'd really like to be.

I think I'd be a glossy cat
A little plump, but not too fat.
I'd never touch a bird or mouse
I'm much too busy round the house.

And then a fierce and hungry hound
The king of dogs for miles around;
I'd chase the postman just for fun
To see how quickly he could run.

Perhaps I'd be a crocodile
Within the marshes of the Nile
And paddle in the river-bed
With dripping mud-caps on my head.

Or maybe next a mountain goat
With shaggy whiskers at my throat,
Leaping streams and jumping rocks
In stripey pink and purple socks.

Or else I'd be a polar bear
And on an iceberg make my lair;
I'd keep a shop in Baffin Sound
To sell icebergs by the pound.

And then I'd be a wise old frog
Squatting on a sunken log,
I'd teach the fishes lots of games
And how to read and write their names.

An Indian lion then I'd be
And lounge about on my settee;
I'd feed on nothing but bananas
And spend all day in my pyjamas.

I'd like to be a tall giraffe
making lots of people laugh,
I'd do a tap dance in the street
with little bells upon my feet.

And then I'd be a foxy fox
Streaking through the hollyhocks,
Horse or hound would ne'er catch me
I'm a master of disguise, you see.

I think I'd be a chimpanzee
With musical ability,
I'd play a silver clarinet
Or form a Monkey String Quartet.

And then a snake with scales of gold
Guarding hoards of wealth untold,
No thief would dare to steal a pin—
But friends of mine I would let in.

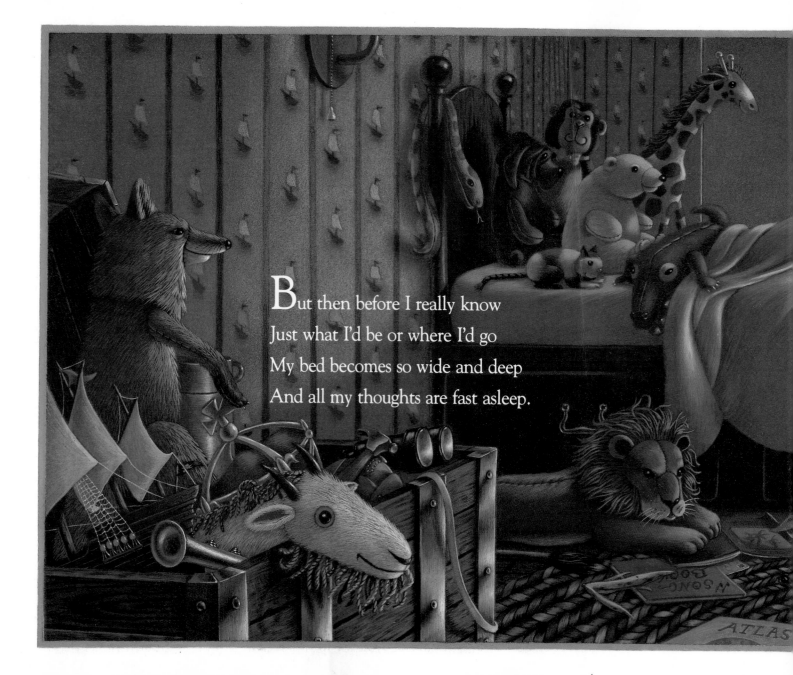

But then before I really know
Just what I'd be or where I'd go
My bed becomes so wide and deep
And all my thoughts are fast asleep.